DATE DUE		
		JUN 0 3 2013		

The Urbana Free Library

To renew materials call
217-367-4057

Tools We Use
Artists

Dana Meachen Rau

Marshall Cavendish
Benchmark
New York

What are all these colors for?

An artist is ready to start painting.

Paint comes in tubes, jars, or cans.

Brushes come in many shapes and sizes.

The artist dips his brush in the paint.

An *easel* holds the picture while he paints.

Some artists draw with pencils.

Some use colorful chalk.

Some artists make *collages*.

They glue down bits of paper.

Some artists do not need paper.

They sew with cloth and thread.

Artists also make *sculptures*.

An artist shapes clay with his hands.

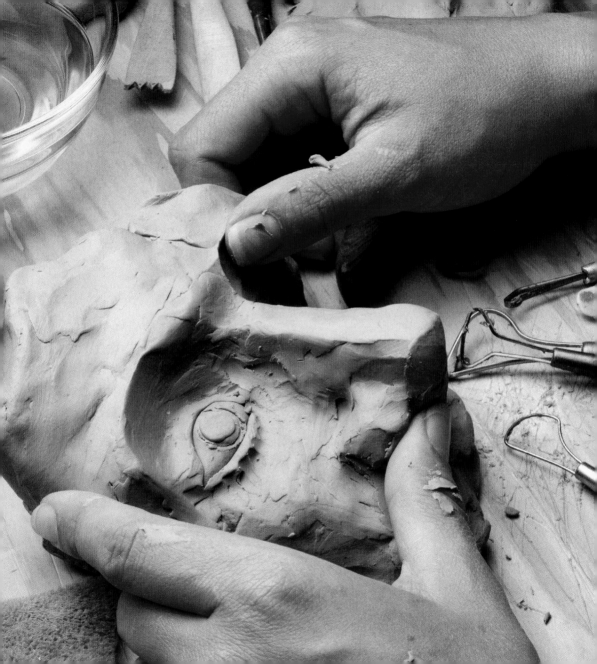

He spins the clay on a wheel.

He cuts the clay with a knife.

Some artists work with metal.

They use fire to melt and join the parts.

A sculpture can be made of stone.

An artist breaks off pieces with a *chisel*.

An artist can use wood to make a sculpture.

He carves the wood with a knife.

You can be an artist.

You can draw a picture with crayons.

You can make a sculpture with paper, paste, and paint.

Imagination is your most important tool.

Tools Artists Use

brushes

chisel

easel

knife

paint   **pencil**   **wheel**

Challenge Words

chisel (CHIZ-uhl) A tool used to chip stone.

collages (kuh-LAZSH-es) Pictures made of pieces of paper or other items glued together.

easel (EE-zuhl) A stand that holds a painting.

sculptures (SKULP-chuhrs) Art that is shaped out of wood, stone, metal, clay, or wax.

Index

Page numbers in **boldface** are illustrations.

About the Author

Dana Meachen Rau is an author, editor, and illustrator. A graduate of Trinity College in Hartford, Connecticut, she has written more than one hundred fifty books for children, including nonfiction, biographies, early readers, and historical fiction. She lives with her family in Burlington, Connecticut.

With thanks to the Reading Consultants:

Nanci Vargus, Ed.D., is an Assistant Professor of Elementary Education at the University of Indianapolis.

Beth Walker Gambro received her M.S. Ed. Reading from the University of St. Francis, Joliet, Illinois.

Marshall Cavendish Benchmark
99 White Plains Road
Tarrytown, New York 10591-9001
www.marshallcavendish.us

Library of Congress Cataloging-in-Publication Data

Rau, Dana Meachen, 1971–
Artists / by Dana Meachen Rau.
p. cm. — (Bookworms. Tools we use)
Summary: "Introduces the tools artists use in their work"—Provided by publisher.
Includes index.
ISBN 978-0-7614-2655-4
1. Artists' tools—Juvenile literature. 2. Artists' materials—Juvenile literature. I. Title. II. Series.
N8543.R38 2007
702'.8—dc22
2006035142

Editor: Christina Gardeski
Publisher: Michelle Bisson
Designer: Virginia Pope
Art Director: Anahid Hamparian

Photo Research by Anne Burns Images

Cover Photo by *SuperStock*/Roger Allyn Lee

The photographs in this book are used with permission and through the courtesy of:
SuperStock: pp. 1, 17, 29R age fotostock; p. 15 SuperStock. *Corbis*: pp. 3, 29L Corbis;
pp. 5, 28TL Gregor Schuster/zefa; pp. 7, 28BL Ashley Cooper; pp. 9, 29C Patrick Ward;
p. 11 Gabe Palmer/zefa; p. 19 Layne Kennedy; pp. 21, 23, 28TR, 28BR Peter Beck;
p. 25 Laura Dwight; p. 27 Jose Luis Pelaez, Inc.
Woodfin Camp: p. 13 John Eastcott & Yva Momatiuk.

Printed in Malaysia
1 3 5 6 4 2